This book belongs to:

____

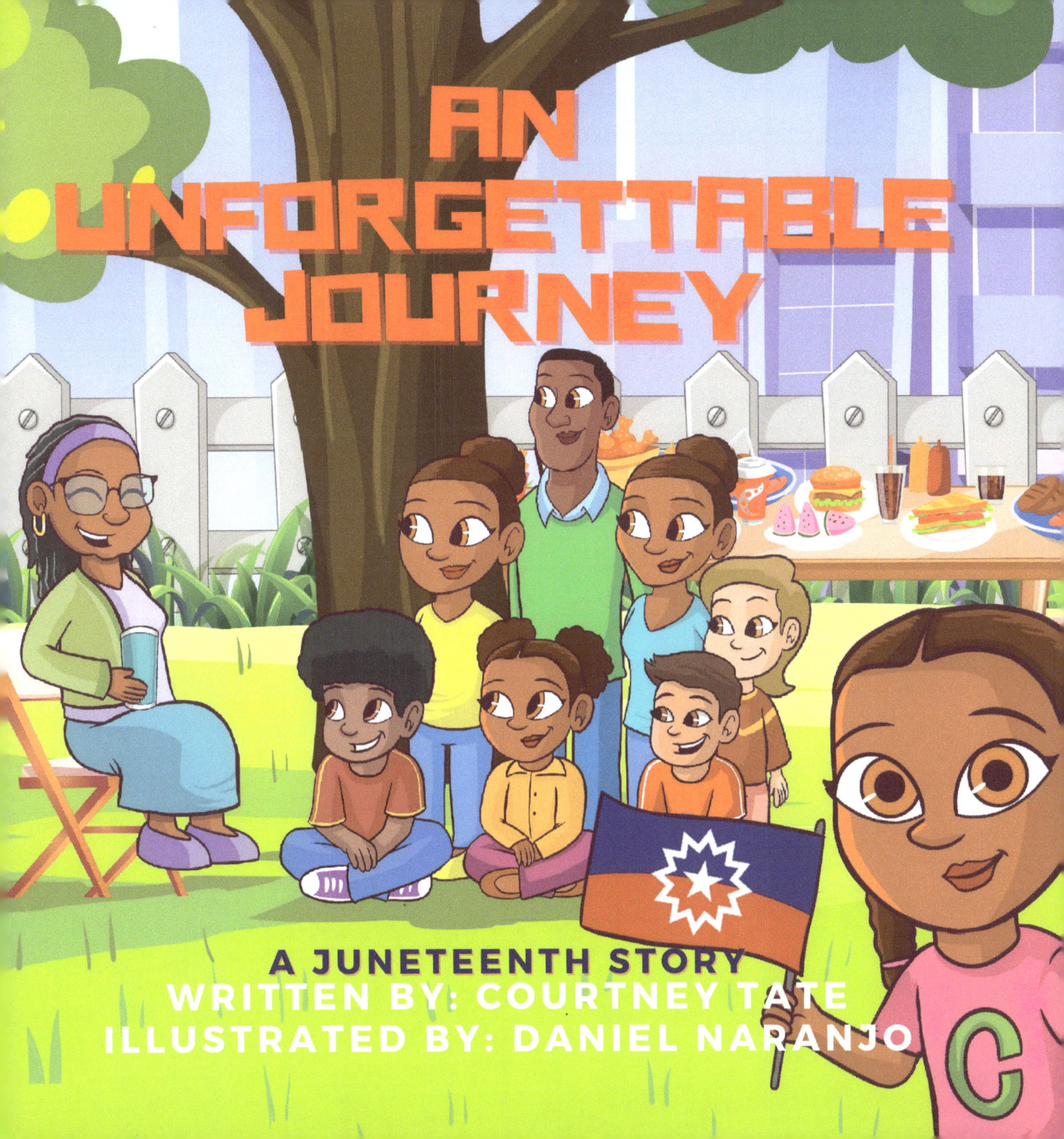

AN UNFORGETTABLE JOURNEY
A JUNETEENTH STORY
WRITTEN BY: COURTNEY TATE
ILLUSTRATED BY: DANIEL NARANJO

The sounds of laughter and excitement filled the air as the children played on the swings and splashed through the water. The Juneteenth cookout was finally here. Campbell had waited for this all year long and was surrounded by all of her friends and cousins.

Campbell and the other children smelled the delicious food on the grill all afternoon long. "The food is ready!" someone shouted, and all of the children cleaned up and raced each other to the food line as fast as they could!

There were so many tasty options on the table that Campbell's tummy rumbled and growled for the feast to come. There were hamburgers, hotdogs, fried fish, chicken wings, corn on the cob, baked beans, fresh fruit, and so much more! Campbell's plate was so full that she rushed to the table before the flimsy paper thing could fold under all that weight. Everyone at the table licked their lips, ready to throw down!

With everyone finishing up their food and throwing their napkins on their plates, Campbell and the other children were growing more and more excited by the minute. "Dad, is it almost time?" she asked. Her dad glanced down at his watch. "Yup, it's time!" he said.

"Yes!" Campbell shouted with joy. "Everyone, come on. It's story time!" All of the children raced behind her toward the big tree and took their seats.

Each year, Ms. Sarah told a story at
the cookout, and since they were
celebrating Juneteenth this year,
Campbell knew it was going to be EPIC!
"All right, everyone," Campbell said,
standing in front of the crowd. "This
is Ms. Sarah. She's going to tell us an
awesome story today!"

"Girl, we all know Ms. Sarah. She needs no introduction!" someone shouted from the crowd as everyone laughed. Ms. Sarah was well known in the community. She had been around for a long time and was filled with wisdom and enthusiasm. Campbell just couldn't hide her excitement to hear the day's story.

Ms. Sarah took her seat holding her glass of ice-cold sweet tea right beside her. "All right, boys and girls, are y'all ready for a story?" she said with a smile, and all the children cheered! "Whew, I am just so excited that it is Juneteenth. I never thought I would see the day that we would celebrate it as a national holiday," Ms. Sarah said, waving her hand.

"My grandpa used to tell us stories under a tree, just like we are today," she recalled. "And now I get to share those stories with you all." The children crossed their legs and focused all their attention on Ms. Sarah.

"Once a long time ago, black men and women were sold into slavery and forced to work in the fields. The women often cooked and cleaned and weren't allowed to learn how to read. Meanwhile, men were forced to do manual labor. Everything from plowing fields to building houses. These were very hard times. Black men and women didn't have freedom like we do today. Until one significant day, when President Abraham Lincoln signed the Emancipation Proclamation that was said to free all slaves..

"All over the nation, there were celebrations and cheer! Black women and men dreamed of the day that they could live lives of their own. But even after the Emancipation Proclamation, in many parts of Texas, they were still plowing the fields all day long in that heat and working as slaves.

"However, two years, five months, and eight days later, a glorious day came for all of the slaves that still only could dream of freedom. On that day, Union Major General Gordon Granger walked through the city of Galveston, Texas, with the following announcement.
"He said, 'The people of Texas are informed that, in accordance with a proclamation from the Executive of the United States, all slaves are free . . .'

"Youngins, you wouldn't believe the excitement. People cried tears of relief and jumped up and down with joy! They hugged their neighbors and ran around with excitement. But most of all, they felt like they could finally breathe. Even if it was just a small moment in time, they felt as if their lives had changed forever.

"At that moment, former slaves and all black people walked the streets with their heads held high. They felt as if finally, they had won. The people gathered together with love and celebrated with delicious food and, most of all, with freedom.

They had waited for that day for so long, and for the first time ever, they could come together and engage with each other, something they had never done before."

Hearing this story made all of the children cheer. They cheered for the black men and women who had won the freedom they deserved. They even cheered for freedom of their own. Ms. Sarah continued, "I remember going to my grandpa's, where everyone in the community gathered together every year to celebrate that day of freedom now known as Juneteenth.

"Black people and white people were still separated back then, even going to completely different schools based on color. Black people still weren't allowed to be in the same spaces as white people, but Juneteenth represented freedom. It represented progress.

"Each Juneteenth we would go to the parade and dance in the streets, celebrating the freedom of our ancestors. Then we would go to recreation centers or church and eat real good. We really threw down then! We would laugh together, play, and run around just like you all are today, except it was just black folks gathering in celebration.

"'Today is freedom day. It's OUR freedom day!' we used to chant."
Ms. Sarah leaned back in her seat and drank a sip of her sweet tea.
"That's my story of how we came to celebrate today, Juneteenth,
freedom day," she said. With a big smile, she glanced at all of the
children of various ethnicities and colors sitting in front of her and
felt true happiness in her heart. Quietly and joyfully, she resumed
the chant from her childhood.

"Today is freedom day. It's OUR freedom day!" she said, and the children all stood up, jumping with excitement. "Today is freedom day. It's our freedom day!" the children began to chant over and over again as they danced, laughed, and celebrated freedom together. "Juneteenth is to celebrate freedom. Always remember that!" Ms. Sarah shouted.

Campbell looked around at everyone at the cookout and felt proud. Proud to be celebrating such a great part of history with love, gratitude, and freedom in her heart.

June 19th became known as Juneteenth. African Americans first celebrated their independence on June 19, 1866. The tradition spread from Texas to Louisiana, Arkansas, and Oklahoma. It later spread all the way to Florida, Alabama, and even California.

Some people celebrated by purchasing property and land, a luxury that they had never had before. They would read the Emancipation Proclamation, have marvelous parades, dance, and gather to eat and pray with each other. The children learned from Ms. Sarah that Juneteenth is still a day to reflect and rejoice with family, friends, and the community. As of June 17, 2021, it is officially recognized as a national holiday.

Want to learn more?! Checkout the resources listed below.

https://www.juneteenth.com/
https://www.history.com/news/what-is-juneteenth

Thank you for your support! Follow my
author journey and order more books
on my website.

https://CourtneySTate.com/books

Courtney Tate

About the Author

Courtney Tate is a veteran educator with thirteen years of educational experience. Upon discovering that there were not enough books representing children of color, she seized the window of opportunity and now identifies as an author of children's books. Her books serve a three-fold purpose of educating, entertaining and empowering young children while inspiring them to embrace self-love and build family traditions.

Courtney holds a Bachelor's Degree in Elementary Education from Winston-Salem State University, as well as a Master's Degree in Eexecutive Leadership from Gardner-Webb University. She currently resides in the Charlotte metropolitan area where she serves as an educational consultant.